$23.95

YOUNG ADULT

Essential Literary Genres

BY VALERIE BODDEN

Essential Library

An Imprint of Abdo Publishing | abdopublishing.com

ABDOPUBLISHING.COM

Published by Abdo Publishing, a division of ABDO, PO Box 398166, Minneapolis, Minnesota
55439. Copyright © 2017 by Abdo Consulting Group, Inc. International copyrights
reserved in all countries. No part of this book may be reproduced in any form without
written permission from the publisher. Essential Library™ is a trademark and logo of Abdo
Publishing.

Printed in the United States of America, North Mankato, Minnesota
082016
012017

Interior Photos: Seth Wenig/AP Images, 11; Staff/MCT/Newscom, 12; Aspen Photo/
Shutterstock Images, 15; Bruce Matsunaga CC 2.0, 18; George Ostertag/SuperStock,
21; Shutterstock Images, 26, 43; © Showtime/Photofest, 33, 48; Marcus Donner/
ZumaPress/Newscom, 34; Taylor Hill/Getty Images, 39; Carli Bowman/Shutterstock
Images, 45; Sovfoto/UIG/Getty Images, 56–57; Oleg Konin/Rex Features/AP Images,
60; Galerie Bilderwelt/Getty Images, 63; Alberto Estevez/EFE/Newscom, 67; Gonzales
KRT/Newscom, 68–69; Mindaugas Kulbis/AP Images, 76; Twentieth Century Fox Film
Corporation/Photofest, 81, 86, 91, 95, 97; Andy Kropa/Invision/AP Images, 82

Editor: Melissa York
Series Designer: Maggie Villaume

PUBLISHER'S CATALOGING-IN-PUBLICATION DATA

Names: Bodden, Valerie, author.
Title: Young adult / by Valerie Bodden.
Description: Minneapolis, MN : Abdo Publishing, 2017. | Series: Essential
    literary genres | Includes bibliographical references and index.
Identifiers: LCCN 2016945211 | ISBN 9781680783841 (lib. bdg.) |
    ISBN 9781680797374 (ebook)
Subjects: LCSH: Literature--Juvenile literature. | Literary form--Juvenile
    literature.
Classification: DDC 809--dc23
LC record available at http://lccn.loc.gov/2016945211

CONTENTS

LITERARY GENRES

Why do we read and write literature? Telling stories is an integral part of being human, a universal experience across history and cultures. Literature as we know it today is the written form of these stories and ideas. Writing allows authors to take their readers on a journey that crosses the boundaries of space and time. Literature allows us to understand the experiences of others and express experiences of our own.

What Is a Genre?

A genre is a specific category, or type, of literature. Broad genres of literature include nonfiction, poetry, drama, and fiction. Smaller groupings include subject-based genres such as mystery, science fiction, romance, or fantasy. Literature can also be classified by its audience, such as young adult (YA) or children's, or its format, such as a graphic novel or picture book.

What Are Literary Theory and Criticism?

Literary theory gives us tools to help decode a text. On one level, we can examine the words and phrases the author uses so we can interpret or debate his or her message. We can ask questions about how the book's structure creates an effect on the reader, and whether this is the effect the author intended. We can analyze symbolism or themes in a work. We can dive deeper by asking how a work either supports or challenges society and its values or traditions.

You can look at these questions using different criticisms, or schools of thought. Each type of criticism asks you to look at the work from a different perspective. Perhaps you want to examine what the work says about the writer's life or the time period in which the work was created. Biographical or historical criticism considers these questions. Or perhaps you are interested in what the work says about the role of women or the structure of society. Feminist or Marxist theories seek to answer those types of questions.

How Do You Apply Literary Criticism?

You write an analysis when you use a literary or critical approach to examine and question a work. The theory you choose is a lens through which you can view the work, or a springboard for asking questions about the work. Applying a theory helps you think critically. You are free to question the work and make an assertion about it. If you choose to examine a work using racial criticism, for example, you may ask questions about how the work challenges or upholds racial structures in society. Or you may ask how a character's race affects his or her identity or development throughout the work.

Forming a Thesis

Form your questions and find answers in the work or other related materials. Then you can create a thesis. The thesis is the key point in your analysis. It is your argument about the work based on the school of thought you are using. For example, if you want to approach a work using feminist criticism, you could write the following thesis: The character of Margy in Sissy Johnson's *Margy Sings the Blues* uses her songwriting to subvert traditional gender roles.

HOW TO MAKE A THESIS STATEMENT

In an analysis, a thesis statement typically appears at the end of the introductory paragraph. It is usually only one sentence long and states the author's main idea.

Providing Evidence

Once you have formed a thesis, you must provide evidence to support it. Evidence will usually take the form of examples and quotations from the work itself, often including dialogue from a character. You may wish to address what others have written about the work. Quotes from these individuals may help support your claim. If you find any quotes or examples that contradict your thesis, you will need to create an argument against them. For instance: Many critics claim Margy's actions uphold traditional gender roles, even if her songs went against them. However, the novel's resolution proves Margy had the power to change society through her music.

HOW TO SUPPORT A THESIS STATEMENT

An analysis should include several arguments that support the thesis's claim. An argument is one or two sentences long and is supported by evidence from the work being discussed. Organize the arguments into paragraphs. These paragraphs make up the body of the analysis.

Concluding the Essay

After you have written several arguments and included evidence to support them, finish the essay with a conclusion. The conclusion restates the ideas from the

HOW TO CONCLUDE AN ESSAY

thesis and summarizes some of the main points from the essay. The conclusion's final thought often considers additional implications for the essay or gives the reader something to ponder further.

In This Book

In this book, you will read summaries of works, each followed by an analysis. Critical thinking sections will give you a chance to consider other theses and questions about the work. Did you agree with the author's analysis? What other questions are raised by the thesis and its arguments? You can also see other directions the author could have pursued to analyze the work. Then, in the Analyze It section in the final pages of this book, you will have an opportunity to create your own analysis paper.

Young Adult Literature

The book you are reading focuses on young adult literature. Young adult novels generally feature protagonists ages 12 to 18 years and deal with the unique problems and experiences of being a teenager and growing up. Often, adults play only minor roles in these books as teens work through their problems on their own. According to young adult author Jennifer Lynn Barnes, the popularity of young adult literature stems in part from the fact that "teens are caught between two worlds, childhood and adulthood, and in YA [young adult novels], they can navigate those two worlds."[1]

The first books targeted specifically to a teen audience were written in the 1940s, but since then, young adult literature has exploded in popularity. Books written for young adults can fall into any genre, including contemporary, historical fiction, science fiction, fantasy, mystery, thriller, horror, and romance. Common themes in young adult literature include identity, good and evil, family, and first love.

LOOK FOR THE GUIDES

Throughout the chapters that analyze the works, thesis statements have been highlighted. The box next to the thesis helps explain what questions are being raised about the work. Supporting arguments have also been highlighted. The boxes next to the arguments help explain how these points support the thesis. The conclusions are also accompanied by explanatory boxes. Look for these guides throughout each analysis.

2

AN OVERVIEW OF
THE ABSOLUTELY TRUE DIARY OF A PART-TIME INDIAN

American Indian author Sherman Alexie's novel *The Absolutely True Diary of a Part-Time Indian* is based in part on his childhood experiences growing up on an American Indian reservation and attending a white high school in a nearby town.

The story's protagonist is Arnold Spirit (known as Junior to most people on the reservation), a 14-year-old living in the town of Wellpinit on the Spokane Indian Reservation in Washington State. Arnold was born with hydrocephalus, which has left him with numerous physical problems, including seizures, extra teeth, poor eyesight, and a stutter and lisp.

Author Sherman Alexie accepted a National Book Award for *The Absolutely True Diary of a Part-Time Indian* in 2007.

The Spokane Indian Reservation is located in the east-central part of Washington.

These problems have made Arnold the target of major bullying. To stay safe, Arnold spends most of his time at home, reading and drawing cartoons—many of which illustrate the novel (drawn by illustrator Ellen Forney). Arnold's family lives in poverty, and he sometimes goes an entire day without food. His father struggles with alcoholism, and his mother is in recovery.

High School

Arnold is excited for his first day of high school on the reservation, especially geometry class. But when his teacher, Mr. P, hands out the textbooks, Arnold sees his mother's name inside his book. Realizing his geometry book is at least 30 years older than he is sends Arnold over the edge. He throws the book, hitting Mr. P in the face.

During Arnold's ensuing suspension, Mr. P comes to visit. He forgives Arnold and tells him he needs to get off the reservation. That night, Arnold tells his parents he wants to go to Reardan, the all-white high school 22 miles (35 km) from the reservation.

The hardest part of Arnold's decision is telling his best friend, Rowdy. When he does tell him, Rowdy— who has always protected Arnold from bullies—punches him and calls him names.

The Only Other Indian at Reardan

At Reardan, the only other Indian is the mascot. Although most of the students ignore Arnold, some of the jocks call him names. When a senior named Roger tells a racist joke, Arnold punches him. After, Roger walks away. Arnold is dumbfounded—and scared. He figures Roger will plot his revenge because that is what would happen on the reservation. Instead, Roger is friendly to him the next day at school.

For Halloween, Arnold dresses as a homeless person. So does the prettiest girl at Reardan, Penelope. She is going to trick-or-treat to collect spare change for the homeless, so Arnold decides to do the same thing on the reservation. He raises approximately ten dollars, but three guys assault him and take the money. They want to remind him he is a traitor to his people.

At school, the other students mostly ignore Arnold, as do his teachers. Some days, Arnold's parents don't have enough gas money, so he has to walk or hitchhike to and from school. One day, Arnold works up the nerve to approach Gordy, a social outcast at Reardan, and announces he would like to be friends. After that, the two of them study together, although Arnold knows they will never be best friends like he was with Rowdy. Soon afterward, Arnold begins dating Penelope, which makes him suddenly popular. He learns that Penelope has bulimia and that she feels trapped in Reardan. She dreams of escaping the small town to fulfill her own dreams of becoming an architect.

One day, Arnold returns home from school to find his mother crying. She says his sister, Mary, has gotten married and run away to Montana. She had been living in their basement after giving up her dream of writing romance novels. Arnold knows he should be upset,

An Indian mascot at Reardan contributes to Arnold's feelings of isolation.

but he feels happy for her. Now it is as if she is living a
romance novel, not just dreaming of writing one.

Full-Court Showdown

As basketball season approaches, Arnold considers not
trying out, but his father convinces him to. Arnold has
to face Roger one-on-one. Roger knocks him down a
couple of times, but Arnold manages to score on him.
Coach puts Arnold on the varsity team.

For the first game of the season, Reardan faces the
team from Wellpinit High. As Arnold walks into the
Wellpinit gym, the crowd of his fellow reservation
residents chants, "Ar-nold sucks!"[1] In the third quarter,
Coach puts Arnold in the game. Arnold goes for a layup,
but Rowdy jabs his elbow into Arnold's head, knocking
him unconscious. Reardan loses the game. The coach
sits up with Arnold all night at the hospital, and the
two bond.

Death in the Family

After Christmas, Arnold's grandmother is walking home
when she is hit by a drunk driver and killed. Almost
2,000 Indians show up for her wake. Afterward, the
residents of the reservation sympathize with Arnold

more. They stop calling him names and causing trouble for him.

Not long after, Arnold's dad's best friend, Eugene, is shot in the face and killed. The shooter was one of Eugene's friends, who was extremely drunk. Depressed, Arnold stops going to school for several weeks. When he finally returns, he is mocked by his social studies teacher, who introduces him to the class as a "special guest" because he has been gone so much.[2] Arnold wants to fight back but cannot find the energy. Instead, Gordy gets up and drops his book to protest. Penelope, Roger, and the rest of the class do the same, then they walk out of the room. Arnold laughs, and then he follows them, feeling "a little bit of joy" at last.[3]

Rematch

Meanwhile, Arnold continues playing basketball and becomes a starter. Soon they face off against the reservation team again, this time in Reardan. With 2,000 people in the stands, the coach assigns Arnold to guard Rowdy. Although Arnold is nervous, the coach tells him he believes in him. In the first play of the game, Rowdy intercepts a pass and charges for the net. Arnold knows Rowdy will go for a dunk, and he is

Sherman Alexie is a member of the Spokane and Coeur D'Alene tribes.

ready for it. As Rowdy goes up, so does Arnold, and for the first time, he reaches higher than Rowdy. Arnold steals the ball and takes off down the court, making a three-pointer. Reardan wins the game by 40 points.

Another Death

One day after basketball season ends, Arnold finds out at school his sister is dead. Arnold's dad later tells him that Mary and her husband got drunk and passed out in their trailer, and there was a fire. The trailer burned down with Arnold's sister inside.

During the funeral, Rowdy tells Arnold that it's Arnold's fault Mary died. Arnold worries that maybe he's right because if he hadn't left, maybe his sister wouldn't have left either. The day after Mary's funeral, Arnold returns to Reardan and is astounded by the support of his white classmates and teachers.

Many Tribes

As Arnold thinks of all the loved ones he has lost—he has been to 42 funerals in 14 years—he decides to make a better life for himself. He realizes he belongs not only to his Indian tribe, but also to all kinds of other tribes based on what he does and who he is.

After the school year ends, Arnold spends his days on the reservation, not doing much. He misses his white friends. Then one day, Rowdy shows up and invites Arnold to shoot hoops. Rowdy tells Arnold he has always known Arnold would leave, and he is happy for him. The two play one-on-one until the moon comes up, and they do not keep score.

3

NAVIGATING RACE AND IDENTITY

Searching for identity is a common theme in young adult literature. As young adults grow up, they attempt to define who they are and where they belong in society. For many—especially those belonging to marginalized groups—this search can be complicated by race. How does their race define them? How much are they shaped by it? How does society view them in light of their race? Critical race theory examines cultural perceptions of race. It looks at how social systems and ideas about race shape an individual's identity.

When Arnold Spirit, protagonist of *The Absolutely True Diary of a Part-Time Indian*, decides to leave the Wellpinit reservation to attend all-white Reardan High

A Spokane man wears traditional clothes at a pow wow on the Spokane Indian Reservation. Arnold grows to realize he belongs to many types of tribes.

School, he has no idea the identity crisis it will cause him. He suddenly feels "half Indian in one place and half white in the other."[1] Most of all, he feels alone in both places. In time, however, as Arnold embraces and rejects aspects of both the American Indian and white cultures, he moves from feeling isolated in each culture to forging an individual identity apart from race.

From the beginning, Arnold feels like an outsider even among fellow American Indians and frankly admits the difficult realities of reservation life. Born with hydrocephalus, Arnold has long been an easy target for bullies. But being beat up and called names are not the worst things about life on the reservation—poverty is. Arnold wants to be angry with his parents for being poor, but he knows they "came from poor people who came from poor people who came from poor people, all the way back to the very first poor people."[2] The worst thing about poverty is that it leads to hopelessness, as you "feel that you somehow *deserve* to be poor" because you're Indian and that because you're Indian, "you're destined to be poor."[3] Many people on the reservation have given up their dreams. Arnold's mother, for example, would have gone to college, and his father would have been a musician. Without dreams, many of the people on the reservation turn to alcohol. Arnold estimates 90 percent of the funerals he has attended were because of alcohol. What he has seen on the reservation shows Arnold he needs to get away. He cannot avoid being poor, but he can stay away from alcohol, and he can hold on to his hope for a better life.

Arnold looks to the white world for hope but initially finds himself just as isolated as he is on the reservation. Arnold asks his parents: Who has the most hope? They reply, "white people," leading Arnold to reflect, "I don't know if

ARGUMENT TWO

Next, the author compares Arnold's expectations for the white world to the reality he experiences. She writes, "Arnold looks to the white world for hope but initially finds himself just as isolated as he is on the reservation."

hope is white. But I do know that hope for me is like some mythical creature."[4] He almost thinks of the white kids from Reardan as mythical creatures, too. He calls them "magnificent" and "filled with hope."[5] Their school has things reservation students cannot even dream of: a computer room, a chemistry lab, two gyms. Arnold decides he wants those opportunities—that hope—for himself. Arnold knows it will not be easy and that the town is full of racists. But he is not prepared for the extent of isolation he initially experiences. The first day, the other students stare at him as if he is an alien. As he continues to be isolated, he starts to wonder whether he is, in fact, human.

ARGUMENT THREE

In the third argument, the author shows how experiencing these two cultures affects Arnold: "Living on the reservation while attending Reardan leaves Arnold feeling split, as though he has two different identities."

Living on the reservation while attending Reardan leaves Arnold feeling split, as though he has two different identities. Arnold draws a cartoon of himself split down the middle. One side of him is white, and the other is Indian. The white side has nice, new clothes, "a bright future," "positive role models," and "hope." The Indian side has cheap clothes, "a vanishing past," "a family history of diabetes and cancer," and "bone-crushing reality."[6] Even his names are different in his two worlds. On the reservation, Arnold is known as Junior, just like countless other Indian males. But in Reardan, people laugh at the name Junior. They use his actual name, Arnold Spirit. He tries to explain to Penelope that, "My name is Junior. . . . And my name is Arnold. It's Junior and Arnold. I'm both."[7] But he never feels as though he can be both at the same time.

His identities collide on the basketball court in the first game against Wellpinit. When he arrives at the game, the people from the reservation chant, "Ar-nold sucks!" Arnold is especially struck by the fact that "they weren't calling me by my rez name, Junior. Nope, they were calling me by my Reardan name."[8] The lack of hope on the reservation means people there do not self-identify as successful. They think Arnold is acting white, and this makes Arnold a traitor in their eyes. Later, during the rematch against Wellpinit, the deafening cheers of the Reardan crowd make Arnold feel like "one of those Indian scouts who led the U.S. Cavalry against other Indians."[9] The Arnold side of his identity wants to beat Rowdy, but the Junior side

Meeting Rowdy on the basketball court makes Arnold's identities collide.

worries that the "white people were really interested in seeing some Indians battle each other."[10]

ARGUMENT FOUR

Now the author compares Arnold's experiences with the people in his two worlds: "As he compares the people on the reservation with the people at Reardan, Arnold comes to see the value of both cultures."

As he compares the people on the reservation with the people at Reardan, Arnold comes to see the value of both cultures. He has a father figure in both locations: his dad and his coach. Both support and encourage his dreams and help him believe in himself. He has best friends who look out for and protect him in both places, too: Rowdy and Gordy. The girls in his life also teach him the value of both cultures. His sister Mary didn't achieve her dreams of living a romantic life, but she inspires Arnold by trying. And Penelope shows him that even white kids worry about whether they will be able to fulfill their dreams. In time, Arnold becomes integrated into a larger community both on the reservation and in Reardan. Most of the people on the reservation stop looking at him as a traitor after the death of his grandmother. And after the death of his sister, Arnold's white classmates and teachers show concern for him, making him realize he matters to them, just as they now matter to him. When Arnold makes a list of the people who have brought the most joy to his life, it includes people from both the reservation and Reardan.

Arnold ultimately finds his identity as an individual, apart from his race. Despite the racism and difficulties he has encountered, Arnold knows he is going to have a better life in the white world than he could ever have on the reservation. Yet, he knows he will continue to identify as an American Indian. But more than that, Arnold realizes that he doesn't have to choose between his white tribe and his Indian tribe. He can belong to

ARGUMENT FIVE

The final argument shows how Arnold comes to see himself: "Arnold ultimately finds his identity as an individual, apart from his race."

both and to a whole bunch of others, too, including the tribe of basketball players and bookworms and cartoonists. His race is only one part of his identity, and it doesn't define him more than any other part.

Feeling like part of two separate worlds almost pulls Arnold apart. But by taking hold of what is great from each world, Arnold is able to forge his own identity. That identity stems not only from the reservation and Reardan, but also from who he is as an individual. And because his new sense of identity is intact, readers can be confident Arnold is going to be okay—wherever he goes.

CONCLUSION

The last paragraph concludes the argument by restating the thesis and arguments. It comes back to the idea of Arnold's identity crisis and shows how he has resolved it by forging his own identity.

THINKING
CRITICALLY

Now it's your turn to assess the essay. Consider these questions:

1. Do you agree with the author's thesis that Arnold has forged an individual identity? Is there any evidence that his identity is still largely based on his race?

2. The author states that Arnold fights to hold on to his hope. Do you see any examples of this? Do you think this is what allows him to create his own identity?

3. Does everyone belong to many tribes, like Arnold says he does? Do all of these tribes influence a person equally?

OTHER
APPROACHES

The previous essay is only one example of how to analyze the young adult novel *The Absolutely True Diary of a Part-Time Indian*. Another approach might focus on negative stereotypes in the novel. Yet another option is to examine Sherman Alexie's intent in writing the book.

Negative Stereotypes in *The Absolutely True Diary of a Part-Time Indian*

Although some critics have hailed this novel as a realistic portrayal of American Indian life, others have denounced it for implying all American Indians are poor, violent, and drunk. A thesis for this approach could be: *The Absolutely True Diary of a Part-Time Indian* perpetuates negative stereotypes of American Indian culture and reinforces the message that American Indians need whites to save them.

Author Intent and *The Absolutely True Diary of a Part-Time Indian*

Sherman Alexie once said he does not write to "protect" young American Indians but "to give them weapons—in the form of words and ideas—that will help them fight their monsters."[11] A thesis for this approach could be: By showing Arnold's escape from the hopelessness of reservation life, Alexie encourages young American Indian readers to pursue their own dreams, even if that means living a life different from everyone else in their culture.

OVERVIEWS OF
SPEAK AND WE WERE LIARS

Published in 1999, Laurie Halse Anderson's contemporary novel *Speak* was both a National Book Award Finalist and a Printz Honor book. The story opens on the first day of narrator Melinda Sordino's freshman year of high school. Melinda's friends (including her best friend, Rachel) are no longer talking to her because of something that happened during the summer. Melinda wants to tell them the truth about what happened, but she cannot; her throat burns whenever she tries to speak.

The art teacher, Mr. Freeman, assigns the class an art project that will make a statement about their emotions. Melinda randomly picks the word *tree* for the yearlong project. She decides to attempt a linoleum carving.

Speak was made into a movie in 2005 starring Kristen Stewart as Melinda.

Author Laurie Halse Anderson's books have won multiple awards, and many are best-sellers.

IT

One day, Melinda's social studies teacher tries to stop her in the cafeteria to talk about a late assignment, but Melinda dodges him. She heads for the Senior Wing, where she ducks into an old janitor's closet to hide.

The closet soon becomes her own personal escape—the place she goes to hide when she doesn't feel like going to class.

Melinda is on her way to make her closet feel more homey when her new friend Heather—a girl who recently moved to the area—drags her to the school pep rally. A girl sitting behind Melinda asks if she is the one who called the cops at Kyle Rodgers's party that summer. Melinda wants to explain what really happened but finds she can't say anything.

Soon afterward, Melinda sees a boy she calls only "IT" in the hallways at school. IT smiles at her, and Melinda feels like she is going to throw up. She calls IT her nightmare.

Trouble and Then the Truth

At home, Melinda spends most of her time in her room, communicating with her parents through notes. In art class, Melinda struggles to bring her carving of a tree to life. But it always looks dead. Even so, art is the only class in which Melinda exerts much effort. When Melinda's latest report card comes home, her parents are furious about her grades. That night, Melinda purposely harms herself by scratching at her arm with a paper clip, which she realizes is not so much a cry for help as "a whimper, a peep."[1]

At school, IT—who we now learn is named Andy Evans—torments her, whispering to her and touching her hair. She runs away whenever she sees him. The winter drags on. Heather tells Melinda that she no longer wants to be her friend, saying Melinda is too weird and depressed.

One day, Melinda's lab partner David invites her to a party at his house. Mclinda makes excuses about why she can't go. That night, she thinks about the end-of-summer party that started all her trouble. At the party, Melinda had a few beers and then walked outside, feeling as though she would throw up. Andy Evans, a senior, came up to her and started flirting. He danced with her, and then he kissed her. And then they were on the ground, and he was on top of her. She said no, but he would not get off. When she opened her mouth to scream, he covered it with his hand. Then, "wham! shirt up, shorts down . . . and he hurts me hurts me hurts me and gets up."[2] Melinda ran to the house and called 911, but when the police asked what her emergency was, she couldn't say anything. She fled.

The Warning

After another run-in with Andy, Melinda seeks out her ex–best friend Rachel, who is now dating Andy. Melinda and Rachel write notes back and forth in the library. Melinda writes that she called the cops at the party because Andy raped her. Rachel screams that Melinda is a jealous liar.

Melinda does not go to prom that weekend, and on Monday, she learns Rachel dumped Andy at prom. After school, Melinda decides to clean out her janitor's closet because she doesn't feel she needs it anymore. She is about to leave the room when Andy shoves her back inside and locks the door, pinning her against it. Melinda screams, but Andy covers her mouth, so she grabs a piece of broken glass and holds it to his neck just hard enough to make a drop of blood appear. Andy is speechless.

Melinda spends the last day of school trying to finish her tree project. She finally gets it right—her tree has life, but it still has one sick branch. Mr. Freeman gives her an A+ and says she has been through a lot. Finally ready to speak up, she replies, "Let me tell you about it."[3]

Overview of *We Were Liars*

E. Lockhart's psychological thriller *We Were Liars* was published in 2014. The novel tells the story of 17-year-old Cadence Sinclair "Cady" Eastman, who is part of the "beautiful Sinclair family," in which "No one is a criminal. . . . No one is a failure."[4] But the family's perfection is an illusion. Cady herself used to be pretty, but she says that ever since her accident, she looks sick and suffers migraines.

Summer 15

Cady says her story starts during the summer when she was 15, which she calls summer 15. Cady and her mother spend their summers at Beechwood, the Sinclair family's private island. The island belongs to Cady's grandfather and has a house for each of his three daughters. Cady loves summers there because she can spend time with her cousins Johnny and Mirren, as well as Gat—the nephew of her Aunt Carrie's boyfriend. Gat has dark skin and his family is from India. He stands out from the others, but he fits in well with Cady, Johnny, and Mirren. The adults call the four of them the Liars. Cady and Gat fall in love during summer 15. But something goes wrong, and an accident happens.

Author E. Lockhart's real name is Emily Jenkins.

The Accident

Cady recounts what she knows of the accident: One night in July of summer 15, she went swimming alone, wearing only a camisole, bra, and underwear. Her mother found her half on the beach, half in the water, and took her to the hospital, where she was treated for hypothermia, respiratory trouble, and a head injury. Afterward, Cady's mother took her home to Vermont. Gat never called or wrote.

The next summer, summer 16, Cady's dad insisted on taking her to Europe, which meant she could not go to Beechwood. Afterward, Cady returned home to Vermont and started giving away her belongings—even a picture of her grandmother, who had recently died.

Summer 17

By summer 17, Cady has flashes of what happened during the summer of her accident, but she can't make sense of them. She sees Mirren holding a gas can for the motorboats, Johnny running down the stairs of Clairmont (Granddad's house on the island), and Granddad's face lit by a bonfire. She used to ask her mother about the accident every day, but her mother says she has told her over and over and Cady never remembers afterward, and the doctors say she needs to remember it on her own. She also constantly tells Cady she loves her.

Cady convinces her mom to take her to Beechwood for summer 17. Approaching the island, Cady notices the traditional-looking Clairmont has been replaced by a modern-looking home Aunt Carrie says is called New Clairmont. The tree out front is different too. At the sight, Cady feels a headache coming on.

Johnny, Mirren, and Gat greet Cady once the adults are gone. The three of them are staying alone at Cuddledown, one of the island houses. Cady is surprised to find that she is taller than the others now; they do not seem to have grown. And they are wearing the same clothes they wore two years ago. When Cady confronts Gat about never contacting her after the accident, he apologizes, and they agree to start over.

Life with the Liars

Cady spends most of her time with the Liars at Cuddledown. They do not do much besides watch television, read, and make messes they do not bother to clean up. She and Gat start seeing each other again, even though Mirren warns that it will end badly.

One day, the Liars paddle kayaks to a cave-like section of the shoreline, covered with rocks. Johnny and Gat jump from a high rock into the water, but when Cady says she is going to jump, the others try to stop her, saying she could die. She makes the leap anyway.

Memories of Summer 15

One morning, Cady wakes up, remembering a fire. The fire had burned down Clairmont, and she and the other

Liars had set it. Cady rushes to Cuddledown to confront the other Liars about what she has remembered. Johnny tells her they did it because the aunties were drinking and fighting over grandfather's estate.

Cady remembers more about summer 15. The aunties had tried to force their children to make a play against each other for Granddad's money. Gat had told her that her grandfather did not like him and would not even call him by name because of his skin color. Her mom had ordered her to stop seeing Gat, saying the relationship would jeopardize her family and future.

All of summer 15, the aunts bickered about grandfather's money, until one night all of the adults left the island in anger. Fed up with the family, the Liars made a plan to burn down Clairmont. That night, they "did what we were afraid to do. We burned not a home, but a symbol. We burned a symbol to the ground."[5]

The Twist

Cady goes home to write down everything she remembers, and another memory surfaces: the dogs were trapped inside Clairmont when it burned down. At the memory, she runs out of the house crying. Gat comforts her and tells her there is more. Cady

Cady finally remembers the fire she helped set.

remembers everything. Gat, Mirren, and Johnny all died in the fire. Each Liar was supposed to set a different floor on fire. Cady set the first floor on fire, and then she ran out of the house. The others never made it.

With the realization of what happened comes a wave of grief and remorse and guilt. Cady crawls to her room and cries for how much she cost everyone. When she emerges, she goes to Cuddledown to apologize to the other Liars, but Johnny tells her they were all to blame. The Liars say they can't stay any longer. Then they disappear into the sea.

Afterward, Cady spends time with her family and helps her little cousins find rocks. The next day, she cleans the mess at Cuddledown. She knows she will endure.

5

COPING WITH TRAUMA

Growing up often means learning to deal with traumatic events. The analysis of how a person deals with such events falls into the realm of psychology. Psychology examines not only what people do, but why they do it—their motivations. Psychological criticism analyzes the psychology of literary characters, treating them as if they were real people with their own unconscious desires and motivations.

Every person faces trauma in his or her own way. Some confront it head on, whereas others deny or ignore it. Melinda of *Speak* and Cady of *We Were Liars* at first isolate themselves and ignore the truth about what happened to each of them. But in time, they learn to use healthier coping mechanisms. Ultimately, Melinda and Cady illustrate how these coping mechanisms can be

Both Melinda and Cady are unable to face the terrible events they lived through.

THESIS STATEMENT

The first paragraph ends with the thesis statement: "Ultimately, Melinda and Cady illustrate how these coping mechanisms can be effective short-term solutions to help victims of trauma cope until they are ready to heal." The rest of the essay will show how the characters deal with trauma.

ARGUMENT ONE

The first argument shows one way the characters deal with trauma: "Initially, both Melinda and Cady take the unhealthy route of suppressing or repressing the tragic events they experienced."

effective short-term solutions to help victims of trauma cope until they are ready to heal.

Initially, both Melinda and Cady take the unhealthy route of suppressing or repressing the tragic events they experienced. For most of their stories, the reader does not know what happened to them because the characters either can't remember or can't bring themselves to speak about it. Melinda tries to suppress her memories of what happened to her, but she can't make the memories go away. At the same time, she can't fully admit to herself—or the reader—the details of what happened until more than halfway through the novel. In an effort to deal with what happened to her, Melinda suppresses her voice and stops speaking almost entirely. She constantly feels an ache in her throat, her jaw clenches, and her lips are scabbed from biting them.

Unlike Melinda, who can't forget, Cady can't remember what happened to her. She represses her memories of summer 15 to keep from reliving the painful events. Although she seems desperate to find out what happened, there are hints that she does not really want to know the truth. Every time her mother tells her what happened, Cady makes herself forget it by the next day. Cady knows things on the island have changed, but she does not question too closely what caused the change. Although the appearance of New Clairmont nearly triggers a headache, Cady thinks her reaction has to do with the missing maple tree. She can't admit to herself that she feels this way not about the tree, but about the other Liars. Cady knows she has changed, too. She begins giving away all of her possessions, saying, "I used to be a person who liked pretty things. . . . But that's not me anymore."[1] She convinces herself she is giving away the items to be charitable; much later, she realizes she is doing it to make up for wrongs she has committed.

Without a strong support system, each girl also isolates herself. Melinda's friends

ARGUMENT TWO

In this paragraph, the author illustrates another way the characters grapple with their traumas: "Without a strong support system, each girl also isolates herself."

have all abandoned her because she called the cops at a party. Melinda starts the school year as an outcast. Whenever things get to be too much at school, Melinda retreats to her janitor's closet. At home, Melinda's parents are often absent. They think her silence is a way of "jerking us around to get attention."[2] When Melinda cuts her arms with a paper clip, her mother does not ask what is wrong or if she needs help; instead, she says, "I don't have time for this, Melinda. . . . Suicide is for cowards."[3]

For Cady, the problem is a family that insists on maintaining the illusion of perfection. Because of her family, Cady has been well-schooled in the art of denial.

Melinda has trouble coping after the attack.

When Cady cries about her grandmother's death, her mother demands that she "act normal," saying, "Silence is a protective coating over pain."[4] Cady's entire family is unwilling to speak to her about the accident, and even her little cousins have been forbidden to say anything to her about the other Liars. As a result, Cady separates herself from her mother, the aunties, Granddad, and her little cousins—who are all still alive. She instead spends her time at Cuddledown with the Liars—who are not.

Finally Melinda and Cady turn to healthier coping mechanisms that allow each girl to acknowledge the truth of what happened to her. Melinda's coping mechanism is her art. On her first day of art class, Mr. Freeman says art allows you to "touch that part of you that you've never dared look at before."[5] For Melinda, that part of her is the rape she has not yet fully acknowledged. At first, art is frustrating and confusing, and Melinda feels as though she is stumbling around with no idea how to carve a tree—just like she has no idea how to begin coping with what happened to her.

ARGUMENT THREE

Now the author shows what finally allows the characters to face what has happened to them: "Finally Melinda and Cady turn to healthier coping mechanisms that allow each girl to acknowledge the truth of what happened to her."

As Melinda continues working through her pain and admits to herself that she was raped, she is able to create a tree that has a little life. It has one sick branch, but the tree will survive, just like Melinda.

The Liars serve as Cady's coping mechanism. Because they are dead, the Liars are not really on the island, but Cady has created them as a way to hold on to what she has lost. She goes with them in the kayaks because, "I do not really want to be separate from them. Ever."[6] She will not admit to herself that the only way to be with them is to die. And yet, she thinks about how she would like her ashes spread on the island. She tells Gat she wishes she were dead. She even makes a potentially suicidal jump off the rocks. Through all of this, the Liars protect Cady. They try to stop her from jumping, and Gat yells at her for saying she wishes she were dead. Throughout the novel, the Liars also give Cady little clues about what happened, helping her to slowly let the truth in. For example, they have not grown and are still wearing their clothes from summer 15. Gat tells her that he does not want his ashes on the island, and Mirren listens to song lyrics about wasting youth. When Cady complains that no one will tell her what happened, Gat says, "I think we're telling you, but you can't hear it."[7] After that, Cady remembers the full truth: the Liars are dead, and she is responsible for their deaths.

As each girl faces the truth of her situation, she is empowered to confront what has happened and begin the healing process. Melinda is finally able to call what happened to her "rape." She is not yet able to speak about it, but she writes about it to warn her ex–best friend Rachel. At first she writes that Andy "hurt" her, but then she scribbles that out and calls it what it really was: "rape."[8] When Andy attacks her again in the closet, she finally speaks, screaming loudly. She holds a piece of glass to his neck, wanting to hear him scream, too, but gets something even better. Now he is the one who cannot speak. Ultimately, she realizes that "IT happened. There is no avoiding it, no forgetting. No running away, or flying, or burying, or hiding."[9] She knows it was not her fault and is determined not to let it kill her. She is finally ready to speak.

For Cady, confronting what happened comes in a rush at the end. She has gone through most of the novel

ARGUMENT FOUR

Finally, the author argues that confronting the truth allows the characters to heal: "As each girl faces the truth of her situation, she is empowered to confront what has happened and begin the healing process."

thinking she was the victim of an attack of some sort, but she is faced with the sudden realization that she helped cause the tragedy. Once she gets past crying about what happened, she comes to see she is still loved. Her mother's constant refrain of "I love you" is her way of saying, "I love you in spite of my grief. Even though you are crazy. I love you in spite of what I suspect you have done."[10] Even the aunts, whose children are dead because of what Cady has done, still love her. Once she knows the truth, Cady stops isolating herself from her family and starts spending time with them. She also says goodbye to the Liars, knowing they love her, too, despite everything. When she no longer needs them, they leave her. Cady is still sad and still alone, but she now knows she can cope with what has happened.

Recovery from trauma is a long process for both Cady and Melinda. But by using coping mechanisms to help them overcome their unhealthy responses to tragedy, both girls begin healing. After they confront the truth, they can continue that healing with the support of their families and friends.

CONCLUSION

In the conclusion, the author summarizes the arguments and thesis to show that the girls will be able to move on from their traumas.

THINKING
CRITICALLY

Now it's your turn to assess the essay. Consider these questions:

1. The author argues that coping mechanisms allow Melinda and Cady to deal with their traumas. Do you agree? Is there anything else that might be responsible for helping the characters heal?

2. The author states that Cady imagines the Liars are present during summer 17. Do you agree? Could there be another explanation for why the Liars are on the island?

3. Which argument do you think is the weakest? Which is the strongest? Why?

OTHER
APPROACHES

The previous essay is only one example of how to analyze the young adult novels *Speak* and *We Were Liars*. Another approach might examine how young adult literature can help teen readers understand mental health issues. Yet another approach might examine the unique narrative techniques used in the novels.

Mental Health, History, and Literature

In the past, topics such as depression and mental illness were considered taboo and were often excluded from literature. But today, young adult books are beginning to reflect the reality that 20 percent of teens struggle with mental health issues.[11] A thesis for this approach could be: *Speak* and *We Were Liars* are important additions to the growing canon of young adult books dealing openly with mental health issues and providing teens with positive examples of characters who overcome such challenges.

Narrative Technique in *Speak* and *We Were Liars*

Both *Speak* and *We Were Liars* rely on unique narrative techniques, such as short, choppy paragraphs, stream-of-consciousness, and withholding information. A thesis examining this idea could be: The unique narrative techniques of *Speak* and *We Were Liars* reinforce their characters' states of mind and reflect their ways of seeing the world.

6

AN OVERVIEW OF
BETWEEN SHADES OF GRAY

Ruta Sepetys's 2011 historical novel, *Between Shades of Gray,* is based on the real-life Soviet occupation of the Baltic states of Lithuania, Latvia, and Estonia, which began in 1940. Residents of those countries who were considered anti-Soviet, including doctors, lawyers, artists, and business owners, were deported, sent to prison, or killed.

The novel opens on June 14, 1941, as the Soviet secret police, known as the NKVD, force their way into the home of 15-year-old Lina Vilkas, who lives in Kaunas,

Soviet soldiers occupied the capital of Lithuania in 1940.

Lithuania. They order the family to be out of the house in 20 minutes. Lina, her mother, and her brother, Jonas, rush around the house packing what they might need. In addition to clothes, Lina packs family pictures as well as two books, paper, and pens and pencils. As Lina packs, someone shoves a loaf of bread through her window, but her mother says they must not accept help from anyone to avoid involving others. The bread sparks the first of many flashbacks that Lina has of her life before the deportation. She remembers a day when the bakery owner gave her a free loaf of bread for her father. When Lina asked her father what he had done to deserve the free bread, he answered simply that you should always stand for what is right. Now, Lina's father has not come home from work, and they do not know where he is.

Lina, Jonas, and their mother are loaded into the back of an NKVD truck already filled with other people from their city. A bald man on the truck says they are all going to die and then jumps from the moving vehicle. The NKVD officers stop the truck and throw the man back inside with a broken leg.

The Train Ride

The truck arrives at a train depot, where thousands of Lithuanians are loaded onto cattle cars. The car Lina's family ends up in is crammed with 46 people, including Andrius Arvydas, who is a boy near Lina's age, and his mother. The train remains in the station overnight. Near dawn, Andrius wakes Lina and says that a long train full of men pulled into the station. He says they should try to find their fathers. Andrius, Lina, and Jonas jump off their train car and duck under the other train, crawling from car to car to speak to the people inside. In the seventh car, Lina finds her father. He tells Lina she can help him find them with her art; he will recognize it the same way she recognizes paintings by Edvard Munch, her favorite artist. Andrius sends Lina and Jonas back to the train while he keeps looking for his father. He does not come back all day.

That night, Lina moves to the door of the train car for some air. She hears a noise below and sees Andrius, badly beaten, under the train. She helps him inside, planting "a seed of hatred in my heart" toward the NKVD for what they have done.[1] She vows to draw everything that happens.

The train continues, eventually passing out of Lithuania and into Russia. It stops only once a day to allow one person from each car to fill two buckets—one with water and one with slop to eat. At the stops, people who have died of illnesses contracted in the unsanitary conditions are unloaded as well. The longer the train travels, the more dead bodies are left behind.

As the journey continues, Lina draws a map of the cities they pass on her handkerchief. After six weeks, the train finally stops in a valley in eastern Russia. They have

People lay flowers outside a cattle car used to deport Lithuanians in 1941 during a 2011 memorial ceremony.

reached the Altai region of southern Siberia, thousands of miles from Lithuania. Lina gives her handkerchief to a stranger, asking him to make sure it gets passed along. She imagines it making its way to her father.

Hard Labor

Lina's group is taken to a labor camp, where Lina and her family are shoved into a tiny hut with an Altaian woman named Ulyushka. She yells at them and demands rent.

The next day, Lina and her mother, along with several of the other women, are forced to dig a huge hole with rusty hand shovels. Jonas works making shoes. For their work, they each get 300 grams of bread a day, a little less than 11 ounces. That night, Lina pulls out her paper and writes down everything that has been happening.

The NKVD keep the prisoners up at night, pressuring them to sign documents stating they are criminals. In the morning, Lina and the other women return to digging, supervised by a young NKVD officer named Kretzsky. Later in the day, the commander, named Komorov, forces the women to get in the hole. He kicks dirt on top of them until they are buried.

Finally, Lina hears Kretzsky say something, and Komorov drives away. The women scramble out of the hole.

A Misunderstanding

Later, Lina sees Andrius enter an NKVD building. She looks inside and sees his mother serving drinks to the Soviets. She looks clean and well dressed. A few days later, Andrius gives Lina's family some salami. Lina confronts him, accusing him of getting the food in return for spying for the Soviets. Angry, Andrius says the guards threatened to kill him unless his mother slept with them. He walks away.

Days pass. The NKVD reduces rations and makes the Lithuanians get up every other night to sit in the office. Lina is assigned to carry 60-pound (27 kg) bags of grain on her back. She learns how to steal a little from the bags without anyone noticing. She and the other deportees scavenge the garbage for food thrown out by the NKVD. Because the bald man is still crippled by his leg injury, Lina's mother always makes sure he gets food, even though he constantly complains.

With cold weather and snowstorms pounding the camp, Jonas falls ill with scurvy. Andrius manages to

An anti-NKVD poster from Germany shows Soviet officers, *left*, with dead prisoners in 1942.

steal a can of tomatoes, which he feeds to Jonas. Lina apologizes for jumping to conclusions about Andrius and his mother.

As Christmas approaches, the Lithuanians gather in the evenings to share stories about the holidays. On Christmas Eve, they celebrate together, passing around pictures of their families. On Christmas Day, Lina gives Andrius a portrait she has drawn of him.

A few days later, the commander demands that she draw a picture of him. Although Lina is repulsed, she does it. She is supposed to be rewarded for her drawing with extra food, so she and Jonas go to the kitchen. There, NKVD officers throw a loaf of bread, canned goods, and garbage at them. Lina gets hit in the head by a tin can, but she and Jonas scurry to pick up everything. Andrius arrives and helps them.

Happy Birthday

On March 22, Lina awakes realizing it is her birthday. But Mother and Jonas do not seem to remember. At the end of the day, Jonas tells Lina to hurry to the bald man's shack for news. When she gets there, everyone wishes her a happy birthday. They give her a pad of paper and a pencil. Andrius gives her a book by Charles Dickens. She thinks it is the perfect present and kisses him. During the next days, she looks forward to seeing him.

One day, Andrius tells her that he has learned they are moving people. Her family is on the list. He is not. She tells him she is scared, and he holds her and tells her not to give the Russians anything, "not even your fear."[2] She gives him all of her drawings, telling him to hide them for her. He tells her to keep drawing so the world will know what the Soviets are doing.

Before sunrise the next day, the NKVD round up those who are leaving. As Lina and her family go,

Ulyushka gives them food. Andrius promises Lina he will see her again.

To the Arctic

Lina and the others spend weeks traveling by train, truck, and barge. They make their way up the River Lena and cross the Arctic Circle, finally stopping near the North Pole. To Lina's dismay, Kretzsky has been relocated with them.

The new camp has buildings for the guards and nothing for the 300 prisoners, who have to build their own huts out of sticks, stones, and scattered logs. They live in the huts for weeks, through raging snowstorms. Whenever it stops snowing, they have to work. Lina is assigned to walk to the tree line with the bald man to get logs. One day, he tells her that her family was deported because her father had helped some other family members escape to Germany. Lina thinks back on conversations she had overheard at home and realizes it could be true.

One day, Lina sees her mother talking to Kretzsky and a cruel guard named Ivanov. Ivanov tells Lina's mother that her husband has been shot and killed in prison. As soon as Ivanov is gone, Lina's mother falls on

Kretzsky, crying. After this, Lina's mother's health fails. She dies on January 5.

Soon after, Lina goes to steal some firewood. A drunken Kretzsky spots her. He says he knows she hates him, and he hates himself, too. Then he turns his back and cries. Lina puts a hand on his shoulder and tells him she is sorry. He says he is sorry for her mother.

By February, many of the people in the hut are sick. Jonas has scurvy again. One day, after a storm subsides, a man bursts into the hut. He introduces himself as Dr. Samodurov, an inspection officer. He orders the NKVD to bring fish for Jonas and the others who have scurvy. When Lina asks how he found the camp, the doctor says Kretzsky contacted him.

Epilogue

The novel ends with an epilogue, set in 1995 in Kaunas, Lithuania, as a construction worker digs up a wooden box. Inside, he finds pages of drawings and writings. A letter, written by Lina, says the items were buried in 1954, after she returned to Lithuania with her brother. They had been imprisoned for 12 years. The letter says that, even now, if they spoke of what happened, the Soviets would kill them. So she has buried her story for someone to discover in the future. Lina writes that her husband, Andrius, "says that evil will rule until good men or women choose to act."[3] She hopes her story will lead the discoverer to tell someone so this kind of evil can never take place again.

Author Ruta Sepetys told the story of the Soviet occupation of Lithuania so it would not be forgotten.

7

JUXTAPOSING GOOD AND EVIL

Among the most common themes in young adult literature is good versus evil. New Criticism is a form of literary analysis that can be used to examine a work's theme. New Critics conduct a close reading of a work. They examine how the various parts of the work—such as setting, characters, and imagery—interact to create a unified whole.

Lina Vilkas lives in a world that seems relatively untouched by evil until the Soviet secret police, or NKVD, forcibly deport her family. The ensuing journey brings Lina face-to-face with evil. And yet, against this

Lina is caught between good and evil in *Between Shades of Gray.*

THESIS

The thesis highlights the literary techniques used in the novel and the message they send: "The settings, characters, and motifs of *Between Shades of Gray* feature juxtaposition that shows how good can exist in the face of evil and hope can persist in the face of despair."

ARGUMENT ONE

The first argument focuses on the novel's bleak settings: "Lina's world becomes an ugly place on June 14, 1941, when her family is deported."

harsh reality, Lina also finds moments of goodness. The settings, characters, and motifs of *Between Shades of Gray* feature juxtaposition that shows how good can exist in the face of evil and hope can persist in the face of despair.

Lina's world becomes an ugly place on June 14, 1941, when her family is deported. The deportation comes without warning, as the NKVD bursts into their home and orders them to be ready to leave in 20 minutes. The NKVD officer makes their cozy home into an ugly setting by throwing his burning cigarette onto the living room floor and grinding it into the wood, making Lina think, "We were about to become cigarettes."[1] Things get uglier as the family is herded onto a cattle car, where putrid smells hover over them, lice bite at their hair, and they eat slop. Later, at the labor camp, shacks they must live in are falling apart, and the people become so hungry they scavenge the NKVD's trash for rotting food: "Bugs and maggots didn't deter anyone. A couple of flicks of the finger and we stuffed it in our mouths. . . . We had become bottom-feeders, living off filth and rot."[2] But even this is not the ugliest setting. In the Arctic, Lina finds herself longing for conditions in the labor camp. Here, they live in an even poorer hut that does little to protect them against the frigid weather. Dead bodies are piled outside the huts like firewood.

The ugly settings surrounding Lina are juxtaposed with her memories of life before the deportation. Flashbacks remind Lina of her life in Lithuania. She remembers her cozy home down to the tiniest details, including the decorations on the spoons. Memories of home help sustain Lina despite the ugliness surrounding her. She also remembers her father telling her to stand up for what is right. This memory strengthens her to do the same.

ARGUMENT TWO

The author now highlights the contrast between Lina's new life and her old life. She writes, "The ugly settings surrounding Lina are juxtaposed with her memories of life before the deportation."

ARGUMENT THREE

Next, the author focuses on characters: "The ugly settings of Lina's new life are populated by ugly characters."

The ugly settings of Lina's new life are populated by ugly characters. The ugliest are the Russians, who call the Lithuanians pigs, leading Lina to wonder, "How can they just decide that we're animals? They don't even know us."[3] Among the worst of the Russians is the commander, Komorov, who takes glee in burying Lina, her mother, and some of the other women alive. Later, when Lina finishes a drawing the Russians required her to make, Kretzsky, another guard she despises, rewards her by throwing food at her and laughing when it strikes her. At the Arctic camp, Lina meets Ivanov, who, like Komorov, seems to take joy in the deportees' distress. He delivers the news of Lina's father's death to her mother in the cruelest way possible: "Suddenly, he lifted his gloved hand to his temple, mocking a gun firing. Mother flinched. Ivanov threw his head back and laughed."[4] Ulyushka, the woman Lina, Jonas, and their mother are forced to live with in the labor camp, demands rent from them. As it gets colder, she demands more and more. The bald man from her hometown also angers Lina. He constantly complains that they would all be better off dead, and he never volunteers to do anything for anyone else.

Despite the evil Lina sees in so many people around her, she is surrounded by people who continue to show goodness and love. Throughout the book, Lina's mother serves as the ultimate example of goodness. She treats the bald man kindly and brings him food, even though he shows little gratitude. She gives Ulyushka Christmas gifts. She even talks to Kretzsky kindly and learns his first name. But it is not only her mother who helps Lina find goodness in the face of evil. Some of the characters she had previously seen as evil surprise her with their acts of goodness. Ulyushka, for example, gives Lina's family food when they are being relocated. Dr. Samodurov, the Russian doctor who bursts into their Arctic hut, surprises Lina, too. She flinches when he holds out his hand, assuming he is going to hurt her, but he instead shakes her hand. The doctor's arrival brings out the best in the bald man, too. When the doctor asks him to

ARGUMENT FOUR

The author continues the focus on characters, now looking at those who demonstrate goodness: "Despite the evil Lina sees in so many people around her, she is surrounded by people who continue to show goodness and love."

to help cut up fish for those who are sick, Lina doesn't think the bald man will help anyone but himself. But the bald man immediately agrees, on the condition that the children in their hut are tended first. Perhaps most surprising of all is Kretzsky. When Komorov buries Lina and the women alive, Kretzsky stops the commander. Later, Lina's mother tells her that Kretzsky looked the other way when she sent letters to the nearby village. In the Arctic, Kretzsky purposely drops wood for Lina to steal.

ARGUMENT FIVE

This paragraph transitions to focus on the novel's motif of art: "Just as the characters juxtapose good and evil, the novel's art motif juxtaposes despair and hope."

Just as the characters juxtapose good and evil, the novel's art motif juxtaposes despair and hope. Lina turns to her art as a way to express her feelings. Her favorite artist is Edvard Munch, and she thinks often about his philosophy that you should "paint it as you see it. . . . Even if it's a sunny day but you see darkness and shadows. Paint it as you see it."[5] This is exactly what Lina does, and it brings her comfort and hope. It gives her a sense of purpose, too, as she draws on her handkerchief and then passes it off, imagining it making its way to her father to help him find them. Lina's drawings also provide a record of the horrors she and the other deportees endure.

These literary techniques result in a story that is ultimately hopeful, despite the atrocities it relates. Even in bleak circumstances, Lina finds love with Andrius. That love offers bright moments: he teases her, she looks forward to seeing him, and they kiss. When they are separated, one of Lina's sources of hope becomes Andrius's promise that he will see her again. Through the pain and despair she feels after her mother's death, Lina knows she wants to live to see Andrius again, to see her brother grow up, and to return to Lithuania. Her mother's example gives her the courage to forgive her enemies. When Kretzsky says he hates himself and cries, she tries to convince herself to leave, but instead, she comforts him. Her forgiveness leads Kretzsky to inform the authorities of the atrocities taking place in the deportation camps, ultimately saving the lives of Lina and the others there.

ARGUMENT SIX

Finally, the author shows how the literary techniques work together to create a message of hope: "These literary techniques result in a story that is ultimately hopeful, despite the atrocities it relates."

A monument commemorates the victims of the
Soviet deportations.

For 12 years, Lina remains in captivity. When she
finally returns home, she has a collection of art that
reflects her experience—the good and the evil, the
hope and the despair. She buries her drawings, trusting
that someday they will be
found, and the world will
know her story. Her greatest
hope is that once the world
knows, good will win, and
this kind of evil will never
repeat itself.

THINKING
CRITICALLY

Now it's your turn to assess the essay. Consider these questions:

1. The author argues that *Between Shades of Gray* is ultimately a hopeful book. Do you agree?

2. Do you agree that the art motif adds to the story's theme of hope and despair? Is there any other purpose for Lina's art in the story?

3. Do you agree with the author's assessment that Lina buries her art out of a sense of hope? Or do you see this as an act of despair or cowardice?

OTHER
APPROACHES

The previous essay is only one example of how to analyze the young adult novel *Between Shades of Gray*. Another approach might focus on the novel's moral message. Yet another option looks at the historical events portrayed in the book.

Morals in *Between Shades of Gray*

Ruta Sepetys has said that part of what she wanted to show in *Between Shades of Gray* is that we cannot "categorize things in the extremes . . . good or evil. I think when you peel back the layers, the truth lies somewhere in the shades of gray."³ A thesis for this approach might be: Lina initially sees people as purely good or evil, but her experiences lead her to realize that most people live somewhere in the middle—between shades of gray.

Unknown History in *Between Shades of Gray*

Both the Holocaust and Stalin's reign of terror occurred during World War II (1939–1945), with remarkably similar purposes and results. Yet, although hundreds of books and movies have been written about the Holocaust, the suffering endured under Stalin has received less attention, in part because its victims were afraid to speak out. A thesis for this approach could be: *Between Shades of Gray* breaks the silence surrounding Stalin's reign of terror in the Baltic, using familiar images from Holocaust literature to give readers a context in which to understand this less-known historical event.

AN OVERVIEW OF
THE MAZE RUNNER

Published in 2009, James Dashner's *The Maze Runner* is a dystopian novel set in a postapocalyptic world. It was made into a movie in 2014. The novel opens with the protagonist riding in a dark elevator. The only thing he remembers is his first name: Thomas. When the elevator stops, doors in the ceiling open, revealing a group of 50 to 60 teenaged boys who pull him out, saying, "Welcome to the Glade."[1] Thomas sees he is in a large courtyard surrounded by walls hundreds of feet high. The leader of the boys introduces himself to Thomas as Alby. Another boy introduces himself as Newt.

A young boy named Chuck takes care of Thomas's sleeping arrangements. While Thomas and Chuck talk, screams come from a shack known as the Homestead.

The high walls of the maze make it impossible for the characters of *The Maze Runner* to climb out.

Chuck says Ben got stung by Grievers and is going through the Changing, but he does not explain what this means. Thomas goes to the shack to get answers. Inside, a boy named Gally tells Thomas he is not allowed to go upstairs. Thomas goes anyway. He sees Ben, writhing in pain, with hives and a web of green veins over his skin.

The Tour

Chuck tells Thomas that outside of the walls is the Maze. Thomas watches as several boys run from the Maze back

Author James Dashner penned sequels *The Scorch Trials*, *The Death Cure*, and *The Kill Order*, as well as a prequel, *The Fever Code*.

into the Glade; Chuck says the boys are Runners. Then the walls slide shut. Thomas feels as if the Maze and the Glade are familiar, as if he has been there before. He knows he needs to be a Runner. The next morning, Newt takes Thomas to a window in the wall. Thomas sees a Griever—a horrific mix of animal and machine, the size of a cow, with a saw blade, shears, and long rods poking out of it. Later, during a tour of the Glade with Alby, Thomas sees a beetle blade—a metallic lizard-like creature. Alby says the Creators of the Glade use the beetle blades to spy on the boys.

Alby shows Thomas the Glade and tells Thomas he will get a job soon. Then he shows Thomas the Maze, which has moving walls that make it difficult to map. Alby stops him from entering because the Number One Rule is to stay out of the Maze unless you are a Runner. He says the punishment for breaking the rule is death, though Thomas suspects he is exaggerating. As they talk, the elevator brings a girl to the Glade. She is the first girl ever. She sits up and says, "Everything is going to change."[2] Then she falls back, unconscious. A piece of paper in her hand says, "She's the last one. Ever."[3] When Alby asks if Thomas knows the girl, he says no. But she starts feeling familiar to him.

Afterward, Thomas follows a beetle blade into the forest, noticing it has the word *WICKED* on its back. He loses the beetle blade but finds a graveyard. While he is there, Ben, the sick boy from the shack, attacks him. Alby shoots an arrow at Ben, hitting him in the head. Ben survives the wound and is banished. Thomas is horrified when the Keepers (the boys who lead the various work groups) push Ben into the Maze as the walls close, locking him out of the Glade.

In the Maze

Alby and a Runner named Minho enter the Maze to check out a dead Griever Minho found. By the time the wall is about to close, they still are not back in the Glade. Thomas thinks they should send a rescue party, but Newt says it is forbidden. As the doors close, Thomas sees Minho dragging an injured Alby toward the Glade. Realizing they will not make it, Thomas dives into the Maze to help. The wall slams shut.

Minho tells Thomas he was dumb to break the Number One Rule and now he will die with them. They hear Grievers approaching. Minho runs off. Thomas won't leave Alby, so he lifts the boy and wraps him with the vines that hang from the wall. He works his way up the wall, moving Alby higher. They are 30 feet (9 m) up when a Griever begins climbing the wall. Thomas swings across the vines, leading the Griever away from Alby.

He gets down from the wall and runs through the Maze, chased by one and then four Grievers. Suddenly, a pair of arms grabs him; it is Minho, and he leads Thomas to the Cliff—a spot where the Maze stops at a huge drop off. Thomas and Minho dive aside, and the Grievers fall over the cliff. Thomas and Minho return to the Glade. The others are shocked because no one has ever survived a night in the Maze. They go back for Alby, who is alive, although he soon goes through the Changing. When he later tries to tell the others about what he sees during the Changing, he begins strangling himself, as if someone else is controlling his actions.

The Keepers hold a Gathering to discuss what to do with Thomas. They decide to put him in the Slammer (a jail) for one day as punishment for breaking the Number One Rule. But they also make him a Runner, even though it usually takes months to become one.

Although the girl is still unconscious, she begins talking to Thomas telepathically. She tells him her name

Minho, *left*, and Thomas, *right*, defeat the Grievers and survive the Maze.

is Teresa and that "it was you and me, Tom. We did this to them. To us."[4]

The Ending

Thomas begins training as a Runner, following Minho. Minho explains that the Runners make maps of the wall movements after every day's run. The pattern repeats every month or so, but they have never found an exit. After an exhausting day of running the Maze, Thomas falls into bed. When he is almost asleep, he hears Teresa say, "Tom, I just triggered the Ending."[5]

The next morning, the sun does not come up and the sky remains gray. Thomas and Minho enter the Maze, where they spot a Griever. They watch as it propels itself off the cliff and disappears. The boys throw rocks after it, trying to figure out where it went. Most of their rocks fall. But a few disappear into an invisible opening.

They realize this must be an entrance. They call it the Griever Hole. When they get back, Teresa wakes up. She tells Thomas the Maze is a code and the two of them had something to do with making it.

That night, the Maze doors do not close. The boys fortify the Homestead. When the Grievers arrive, Gally jumps on one, allowing it to kill him. The next day, Thomas looks at the maps the Runners made. He realizes if he stacks up the maps from one day, they form a letter. Eventually, he, Teresa, Newt, and Minho solve the code: "*Float. Catch. Bleed. Death. Stiff. Push.*"[6] But the words do not mean anything to them. Thomas decides he must go through the Changing to solve the code.

The Changing

That night, when the Grievers come, Thomas throws himself at them. He is stung dozens of times before he manages to escape. Afterward, he enters the Changing and is flooded with memories. When he wakes up, he calls a meeting of the Keepers. He tells them what he saw: the Maze is a test to see whether the boys can build a community as they attempt to solve an impossible problem. He says the Creators want those who survive the Maze to do something important.

Then Thomas drops the bombshell: the reason he was able to find the code was because the Creators forced him and Teresa to design the Maze. He says the only way to escape is to get to a computer in the Griever Hole, where they can input the code.

Most of the Gladers agree to the plan. When they are almost to the cliff, the Grievers surround them. The Gladers fight the Grievers so Thomas, Teresa, and Chuck can jump into the Griever Hole. As Thomas fights a Griever, Teresa enters the code into a computer there. The Grievers shut down, and the other Gladers come through the hole. Only half of them have survived.

WICKED

The survivors make their way down a slide and into a huge chamber, where they finally see the Creators. A woman steps forward. She has the word WICKED on her shirt. Next to her is Gally, who apparently faked his suicide on the Griever. Gally tries to talk to the Gladers, but he can't get the words out because the Creators are controlling him. He pulls a dagger from his back pocket and throws it at Thomas. Chuck dives in front of Thomas and is stabbed in the chest and dies. Thomas attacks Gally, and then he cries over Chuck's body.

When Thomas calms down, the WICKED woman says that everything has a reason for happening. Before the Gladers can say anything, a group of men and women burst through the building's doors and shoot the Creators. The Gladers follow the rescuers onto a bus. A woman tells them about sun flares that killed millions and turned much of the planet into a wasteland. The sun flares were followed by a sickness known as the Flare. She says the Gladers were chosen for "the ultimate test" and everything they "lived through was calculated and thought through" by the Creators, who belong to an organization known as WICKED, which is trying to find children who can end the Flare.[7] The woman says her group is dedicated to stopping WICKED from subjecting children to experiments such as the Maze.

The bus finally stops, and the Gladers find themselves at a dormitory with comfortable beds and pizza. For the first time in a while, Thomas feels almost happy. The epilogue consists of a memo from Chancellor Ava Paige. It states that the Trials were successful and that Chuck's murder as well as the so-called rescue were valuable additions to her plan. The test subjects now think they are safe. They will be allowed one night of sleep, and then Stage 2 will begin.

9

UPSETTING THE SOCIAL ORDER

Young adults are still figuring out their place in society.
Often, this is influenced by their social class, including
factors such as wealth and power, or the lack thereof.
Marxist criticism considers how social class is presented
in a work of literature. A critic taking a Marxist
approach might ask questions such as: Who holds the
power in the work? How do characters of different
social classes interact? Does anyone rebel against the
social structure?

In *The Maze Runner*, the boys of the Glade seem
to have an unusual amount of power for teenagers.
They have been placed in the Glade by adults—the
Creators—but those adults have not given them any
rules. Instead, the boys have established their own social
order. But it is not until Thomas breaks the rules of that

Rebelling against the social order, as Thomas appears to do in *The Maze Runner*, is a common theme in young adult literature.

THESIS STATEMENT

The author places the thesis statement at the end of the introduction: "Thomas's actions and the escape may seem like acts of rebellion, but they play directly into the hands of the Creators, proving the WICKED adults ultimately hold the power." The essay will show how the various power structures operate in the novel.

ARGUMENT ONE

The first argument discusses the Gladers' social order: "Although teens are often considered rebellious, the teens in the Glade set up and follow a carefully established social hierarchy with strict rules."

social order that the boys are able to escape. Thomas's actions and the escape may seem like acts of rebellion, but they play directly into the hands of the Creators, proving the WICKED adults ultimately hold the power.

Although teens are often considered rebellious, the teens in the Glade set up and follow a carefully established social hierarchy with strict rules. As Thomas finds out from the moment he arrives in the Glade, a new arrival is at the bottom of the social order. The moment the elevator door opens, Thomas is insulted by boys who have never met him. He doesn't even know what most of the insults mean because the Gladers use slang words he's never heard before, further marking him as an outsider. Newcomers are matched to jobs, and some of the jobs offer more prestige than others. The most elite Gladers are the Runners. A Keeper is in charge of each work group, and together the Keepers meet to vote on important decisions. Above everyone is Alby (later replaced by Newt), the Gladers' informal leader. In addition to a social hierarchy, the boys have established a set of rules that are rigidly followed. According to Alby, the Number One Rule is, "Ain't nobody—*nobody*—allowed in the Maze except the Runners. Break that rule, and if you ain't killed by the Grievers, we'll kill you ourselves."[1] When Ben attacks Thomas, they sentence him to a punishment worse than death—banishment. Alby tells Ben, "If we let shanks like you get away with that stuff . . . we never would've survived this long."[2]

When he arrives in the Glade, Thomas almost immediately begins to question—and break—the rules. On his first day in the Glade, he walks into the room where Ben is going through the Changing, even though several Gladers have told him newcomers are not allowed in there. When Ben is banished, Thomas is the only one who seems upset by it. He cries while the others look on nonchalantly. Later,

ARGUMENT TWO

The next argument looks at how Thomas disrupts the social order: "When he arrives in the Glade, Thomas almost immediately begins to question—and break—the rules."

when Alby and Minho disappear in the Maze, Thomas
suggests a couple of times that they should put together
a search party, even though Newt says it is forbidden.
Finally, Thomas takes matters into his own hands,
running into the Maze to help Minho and Alby just as
the doors shut. His refusal to follow the rules throws the
whole Glade into disorder. Newt says he "turned this
whole place upside down. . . . Half the Gladers think
you're God, the other half wanna throw your butt down
the Box Hole."[3] His stunt ends up earning him a day
in the Slammer—as well as an early promotion to the
position of Runner. It also proves it is possible to survive
a night in the Maze, something their rules had made the
Gladers believe was impossible. It gets them thinking
that maybe some other
things they thought were
impossible—such as solving
the Maze—are possible
after all.

During his time in the
Glade, Thomas comes to
hate the Creators, but he
eventually realizes he is one
of them and that because

ARGUMENT THREE

In the third argument, the author
looks at Thomas's involvement
in the power structure of the
Creators. She writes, "During
his time in the Glade, Thomas
comes to hate the Creators, but
he eventually realizes he is one
of them and that because of his
position in the power structure
he has the key to beating
the Maze."

of his position in the power structure he has the key to beating the Maze. It does not take long for Thomas to develop a loathing for Creators who would place a bunch of kids in a situation like this and wonders who could be so evil. And yet, the longer he spends in the Glade, the more Thomas comes to realize it feels familiar, as does Teresa. When she wakes up, she tells him what he is beginning to suspect: the two of them were somehow

Thomas appears to be beating the Creators, but the opposite is true.

involved with the Creators. This memory enables him to break the code, but he still does not know what to do with it until he subjects himself to the Changing. Afterward, he has access to all the information he needs to get out of the Maze because he now realizes he and Teresa helped design it.

Thomas uses his information to lead the Gladers out of the Maze, only to discover he has played directly into the hands of the Creators, who hold all the power, and have the whole time. Although the boys appear to be independent in the Glade, the Creators are always pulling the strings. They send the supplies, they spy on the boys with the beetle blades, and they control the Grievers. After Alby goes through the Changing and tries to tell the others what he has seen, the Creators force him to attempt to strangle himself. The Creators send Teresa to trigger the ending, which changes all the rules the boys have come to rely on. Suddenly, the sun does not shine, the

ARGUMENT FOUR

In the final argument, the author shows how the Creators ultimately have all the power: "Thomas uses his information to lead the Gladers out of the Maze, only to discover he has played directly into the hands of the Creators, who hold all the power, and have the whole time."

Thomas feels a connection to Teresa that he does not understand at first.

doors to the Maze do not close, and the Glade is no longer safe. Although the Gladers think they are beating the Creators by escaping, the Creators are actually the ones who make that escape possible. If they had not sent Thomas and Teresa, the Gladers never would have found a way out. No one else had the memories needed to recognize that the Maze was a code or to know what to do with that code once they discovered it. When the Gladers finally make it out, the Creator with the WICKED logo on her shirt confirms that the adults are still in control, telling the Gladers that "everything has gone according to plan."[4] Although the Gladers believe that they have finally escaped the Creators after a group of men and women swoops in to rescue them, the reader knows better. The memo from Chancellor Paige in the epilogue makes it clear that even the so-called rescue was part of the Creators' plan. The boys will move on to Stage 2 the next day, still at the mercy of the adults of WICKED.

Although the social order the Gladers have established keeps life in the Glade orderly and under control, it does little to help the Gladers solve the Maze. For that, they need someone with insider knowledge. But even then, their escape, which they see as an act of rebellion, fulfills the Creators' wishes, ultimately leaving the boys at the bottom of the social structure, subject to the whims of WICKED.

CONCLUSION

The last paragraph sums up the arguments and restates the thesis, once again emphasizing the novel's shifting power structures.

THINKING
CRITICALLY

Now it is your turn to assess the essay. Consider these questions:

1. The author contends that the adults ultimately have all the power in the story. Do you agree? Are there any ways in which the Gladers have more power?

2. Do you think the fact that the Gladers can't remember their pasts influences the power structure in any way?

3. The author states that the Gladers could not have solved the Maze without Thomas and Teresa, who were sent by the Creators. Do you agree? Why do you think the Creators sent them?

OTHER
APPROACHES

The previous essay is only one example of how to analyze the young adult novel *The Maze Runner*. Another approach might consider the moral message of the novel. Yet another idea is to examine the story as an allegory.

Morals in *The Maze Runner* and *Lord of the Flies*

James Dashner has said that *The Maze Runner* was influenced by William Golding's 1954 novel *Lord of the Flies*. But instead of a group of boys who kill each other as in *Lord of the Flies*, he wanted to show boys who created an orderly society. A thesis statement for this approach might be: Although both *Lord of the Flies* and *The Maze Runner* depict a group of boys isolated from the world, the two novels present drastically different messages about the nature of good and evil.

The Maze Runner as Allegory

Some critics see *The Maze Runner* as an allegory—a story in which characters, settings, or events have a symbolic meaning. A thesis related to this approach could be: *The Maze Runner* serves as a poignant allegory for the confusion, grief, and hardship often experienced as one develops from childhood to adulthood.

ANALYZE IT!

Now that you have learned different approaches to analyzing a work, are you ready to perform your own analysis? You have read that this type of evaluation can help you look at literature in a new way and make you pay attention to certain issues you may not have otherwise recognized. So, why not use one of these approaches to consider a fresh take on your favorite work?

First, choose a philosophy, critical theory, or other approach and consider which work or works you want to analyze. Remember the approach you choose is a springboard for asking questions about the works.

Next, write a specific question that relates to your approach or philosophy. Then you can form your thesis, which should provide the answer to that question. Your thesis is the most important part of your analysis and offers an argument about the work, considering its characters, plot, or literary techniques, or what it says about society or the world. Recall that the thesis statement typically appears at the very end of the introductory paragraph of your essay. It is usually only one sentence long.

After you have written your thesis, find evidence to back it up. Good places to start are in the work itself or in journals or articles that discuss what other people have said about it. You may also want to read about the author or creator's life so you can get a sense of what factors may have affected the creative process. This can be especially useful if you are considering how the work connects to history or the author's intent.

You should also explore parts of the book that seem to disprove your thesis and create an argument against them. As you do this, you might want to address what others have written about the book. Their quotes may help support your claim.

Before you start analyzing a work, think about the different arguments made in this book. Reflect on how evidence supporting the thesis was presented. Did you find that some of the techniques used to back up the arguments were more convincing than others? Try these methods as you prove your thesis in your own analysis paper.

When you are finished writing your analysis, read it over carefully. Is your thesis statement understandable? Do the supporting arguments flow logically, with the topic of each paragraph clearly stated? Can you add any information that would present your readers with a stronger argument in favor of your thesis? Were you able to use quotes from the book, as well as from other critics, to enhance your ideas?

Did you see the work in a new light?

GLOSSARY

ALLEGORY
A story that teaches the reader a moral or religious lesson.

CONTEMPORARY
Set in the present.

DEPORT
To force someone to leave a country.

DYSTOPIAN
A type of utterly horrible or degraded society that is generally headed to an irreversible oblivion.

HYDROCEPHALUS
A condition marked by excess fluid in the cranium, causing an enlargement of the head and often affecting the brain.

JUXTAPOSE
To put two things side by side for the purpose of comparing or contrasting them.

MARGINALIZE
To exclude a person or group of people or treat them as unimportant or of a lower class.

MORAL
Having to do with ideas of right and wrong.

MOTIF
A recurring theme or idea in a work of literature, art, or music.

POSTAPOCALYPTIC
A period of time following an event that caused mass destruction and much loss of life.

PROTAGONIST
The main character in a book, movie, play, poem, or other work.

PSYCHOLOGY
The study of the mind, emotions, and behavior.

REPRESS
To hold back a thought or emotion or to force painful memories into the unconscious.

STEREOTYPE
An often unfair and untrue belief that many people have about all people or things with a particular characteristic—for example, gender or race.

STREAM-OF-CONSCIOUSNESS
A narrative technique in which the thoughts of a character are written in a continuous flow as they occur.

SUPPRESS
To hold something back or intentionally avoid thinking about painful or unacceptable subjects.

TELEPATHY
Communication between minds, without speaking.

THEME
The subject or main idea of a creative work.

ADDITIONAL
RESOURCES

SELECTED BIBLIOGRAPHY

Alexie, Sherman. *The Absolutely True Diary of a Part-Time Indian*. New York: Little, 2007. Print.

Anderson, Laurie Halse. *Speak*. New York: Farrar, 1999. Print.

Dashner, James. *The Maze Runner*. New York: Delacorte, 2009. Print.

Lockhart, E. *We Were Liars*. New York: Delacorte, 2013. Print.

Lynn, Steven. *Texts and Contexts: Writing About Literature with Critical Theory*. New York: Longman, 1998. Print.

Sepetys, Ruta. *Between Shades of Gray*. New York: Philomel, 2011.

Strickland, Ashley. "A Brief History of Young Adult Literature." *CNN*. CNN, 15 Apr. 2015. Web. 2 June 2016.

FURTHER READINGS

Bodden, Valerie. *Coming of Age*. Minneapolis, MN: Abdo, 2015. Print.

Cart, Michael. *Young Adult Literature: From Romance to Realism*. 3rd ed. Chicago, IL: ALA Neal-Schuman, 2016. Print.

Wilcox, Christine. *Young Adult Authors*. San Diego, CA: ReferencePoint Press, 2017. Print.

WEBSITES

To learn more about Essential Literary Genres, visit **booklinks.abdopublishing.com**. These links are routinely monitored and updated to provide the most current information available.

FOR MORE INFORMATION

For more information on this subject, contact or visit the following organizations:

Balzekas Museum of Lithuanian Culture
6500 S Pulaski Road
Chicago, IL 60629
773-582-6500
http://www.balzekasmuseum.org
The Balzekas Museum of Lithuanian Culture holds the largest collection of Lithuanian artifacts outside of Lithuania.

Martha's Vineyard Museum
59 School Bus Street
Edgartown, MA 02539
508-627-4441
http://www.mvmuseum.org/
In *We Were Liars*, Martha's Vineyard is a short boat ride from the fictional Beechwood Island. The Martha's Vineyard Museum is located blocks from Murdick's Fudge, where Cady buys fudge for Gat.

Northwest Museum of Arts and Culture
2316 West First Avenue
Spokane, WA 99201
509-456-3931
http://www.northwestmuseum.org/
The Northwest Museum of Arts and Culture features the peoples, cultures, and art of the Pacific Northwest. It is located about thirty minutes from Reardan and an hour from Wellpinit.

SOURCE NOTES

CHAPTER 1. INTRODUCTION TO LITERARY GENRES

1. Ashley Strickland. "A Brief History of Young Adult Literature." *CNN.com.* CNN, 15 Apr. 2015. Web. 20 July 2016.

CHAPTER 2. AN OVERVIEW OF *THE ABSOLUTELY TRUE DIARY OF A PART-TIME INDIAN*

1. Sherman Alexie. *The Absolutely True Diary of a Part-Time Indian.* New York: Little, 2007. Print. 143.

2. Ibid. 175.

3. Ibid. 176.

CHAPTER 3. NAVIGATING RACE AND IDENTITY

1. Sherman Alexie. *The Absolutely True Diary of a Part-Time Indian.* New York: Little, 2007. Print. 118.

2. Ibid. 11.

3. Ibid. 13.

4. Ibid. 45, 51.

5. Ibid. 50.

6. Ibid. 57.

7. Ibid. 60.

8. Ibid. 143.

9. Ibid. 182–183.

10. Ibid. 184.

11. Angela Sparks. "Resisting First Nations Stereotypes in Banned YA Novel *The Absolutely True Diary of a Part-Time Indian.*" *U.S. Studies Online.* British Association for American Studies, 2 Dec. 2015. Web. 20 July 2016.

CHAPTER 4. OVERVIEWS OF *SPEAK* AND *WE WERE LIARS*

1. Laurie Halse Anderson. *Speak.* New York: Farrar, 1999. Print. 87.

2. Ibid. 135.

3. Ibid. 198.

4. E. Lockhart. *We Were Liars.* New York: Delacorte, 2013. Print. 3.

5. Ibid. 151.

CHAPTER 5. COPING WITH TRAUMA

1. E. Lockhart. *We Were Liars*. New York: Delacorte, 2013. Print. 45.
2. Laurie Halse Anderson. *Speak*. New York: Farrar, 1999. Print. 114.
3. Ibid. 88.
4. E. Lockhart. *We Were Liars*. New York: Delacorte, 2013. Print. 28.
5. Laurie Halse Anderson. *Speak*. New York: Farrar, 1999. Print. 10.
6. E. Lockhart. *We Were Liars*. New York: Delacorte, 2013. Print. 139.
7. Ibid. 193.
8. Laurie Halse Anderson. *Speak*. New York: Farrar, 1999. Print. 183.
9. Ibid. 198.
10. E. Lockhart. *We Were Liars*. New York: Delacorte, 2013. Print. 214.
11. Kimberli Buckley. "Reality Scoop: Promoting Mental Wellness with YA Literature." *The Hub*. YALSA, 2 Feb. 2016. Web. 20 July 2016.

CHAPTER 6. AN OVERVIEW OF *BETWEEN SHADES OF GRAY*

1. Ruta Sepetys. *Between Shades of Gray*. New York: Philomel, 2011. Print. 55.
2. Ibid. 243.
3. Ibid. 338.

CHAPTER 7. JUXTAPOSING GOOD AND EVIL

1. Ruta Sepetys. *Between Shades of Gray*. New York: Philomel, 2011. Print. 5.
2. Ibid. 185.
3. Ibid. 66.
4. Ibid. 297.
5. Ibid. 215.
6. Booksandquills. "Interview with Ruta Sepetys (*Between Shades of Gray*)." *YouTube*. YouTube, 7 Sept. 2011. Web. 20 July 2016.

CHAPTER 8. AN OVERVIEW OF *THE MAZE RUNNER*

1. James Dashner. *The Maze Runner*. New York: Delacorte, 2009. Print. 3.
2. Ibid. 56.
3. Ibid. 57.
4. Ibid. 184.
5. Ibid. 216.
6. Ibid. 290.
7. Ibid. 366.

CHAPTER 9. UPSETTING THE SOCIAL ORDER

1. James Dashner. *The Maze Runner*. New York: Delacorte, 2009. Print. 45.
2. Ibid. 93.
3. Ibid. 150.
4. Ibid. 353.

INDEX

ABOUT THE AUTHOR

Valerie Bodden has written more than 200 nonfiction books for children. Her books have received positive reviews from *School Library Journal*, *Booklist*, *Children's Literature*, *ForeWord Magazine*, *Horn Book Guide*, *VOYA*, and *Library Media Connection*. Valerie lives in Wisconsin with her husband and four young children.